Blastoff! Readers are carefully developed by literacy experts to build reading stamina and move students toward fluency by combining standards-based content with developmentally appropriate text.

Level 1 provides the most support through repetition of high-frequency words, light text, predictable sentence patterns, and strong visual support.

Level 2 offers early readers a bit more challenge through varied sentences, increased text load, and text-supportive special features.

Level 3 advances early-fluent readers toward fluency through increased text load, less reliance on photos, advancing concepts, longer sentences, and more complex special features.

★ **Blastoff! Universe**

Reading Level: Blastoff! Beginners — Grade K → Blastoff! Readers — Grades 1–3 → Blastoff! Discovery — Grade 4

This edition first published in 2025 by Bellwether Media, Inc.

No part of this publication may be reproduced in whole or in part without written permission of the publisher. For information regarding permission, write to Bellwether Media, Inc., Attention: Permissions Department, 6012 Blue Circle Drive, Minnetonka, MN 55343.

Library of Congress Cataloging-in-Publication Data

Names: Davies, Monika, author.
Title: Venezuela / by Monika Davies.
Description: Minneapolis, MN : Bellwether Media, 2025. | Series: Blastoff! readers: Countries of the world | Includes bibliographical references and index. | Audience: Ages 5-8 | Audience: Grades 2-3 | Summary: "Relevant images match informative text in this introduction to Venezuela. Intended for students in kindergarten through third grade"– Provided by publisher.
Identifiers: LCCN 2024039302 (print) | LCCN 2024039303 (ebook) | ISBN 9798893042368 (library binding) | ISBN 9798893043334 (ebook)
Subjects: LCSH: Venezuela–Juvenile literature.
Classification: LCC F2308.5 .D385 2025 (print) | LCC F2308.5 (ebook) | DDC 987–dc23/eng/20240910
LC record available at https://lccn.loc.gov/2024039302
LC ebook record available at https://lccn.loc.gov/2024039303

Text copyright © 2025 by Bellwether Media, Inc. BLASTOFF! READERS and associated logos are trademarks and/or registered trademarks of Bellwether Media, Inc.

Editor: Suzane Nguyen   Designer: Laura Sowers

Printed in the United States of America, North Mankato, MN.

Table of Contents

All About Venezuela	4
Land and Animals	6
Life in Venezuela	12
Venezuela Facts	20
Glossary	22
To Learn More	23
Index	24

All About Venezuela

Caracas

Venezuela is on South America's northern shore. Its capital is Caracas.

The country is home to **unique** animals and places.

Land and Animals

Coastal **plains** rise into mountains in northwestern Venezuela. A long river cuts through central **grasslands**.

Rain forests are found in the southern **highlands**.

rain forest

Angel Falls

Size: 3,212 feet (979 meters) tall
Famous For: the world's highest waterfall

Venezuela is a warm country.
It has a wet and a dry season.

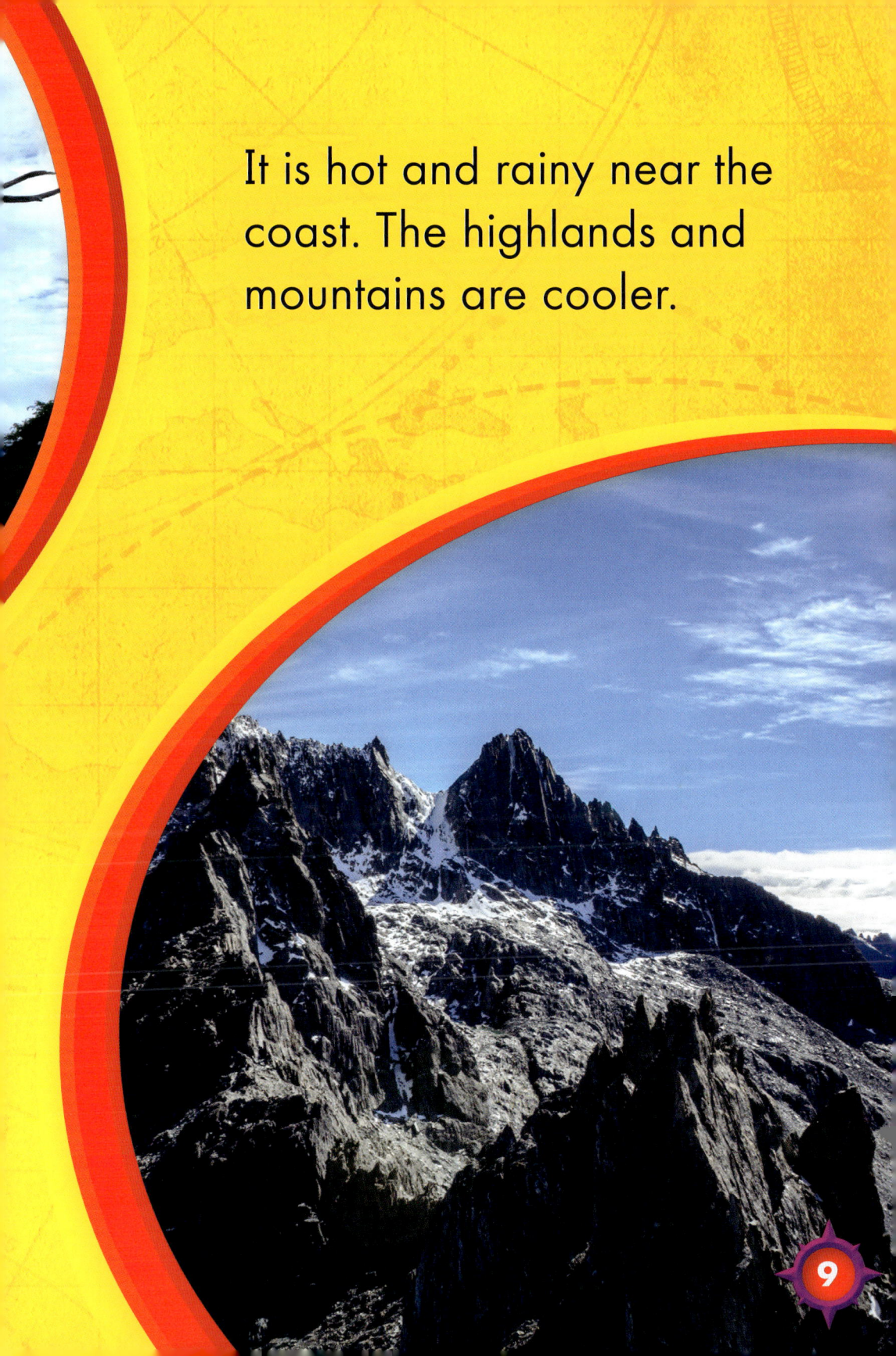

It is hot and rainy near the coast. The highlands and mountains are cooler.

Many animals live in Venezuela. Howler monkeys call from the treetops. Jaguars hunt below.

jaguar

Piranhas attack fish in rivers. Troupials fly overhead.

Life in Venezuela

Venezuelans come from many **backgrounds**. Most speak Spanish. But over 25 **indigenous** languages are also spoken. Many people are **Roman Catholic**.

Venezuelans mainly live in cities.

Roman Catholic church

joropo dance

Music is heard across Venezuela. *Joropo* is the national song and dance.

Baseball and soccer are favorite sports. Many people also enjoy watching soap operas called *telenovelas*.

baseball

soccer

An *arepa* is a corn cake with fillings. *Pabellón criollo* is a dish with beef, beans, and rice.

Venezuelan Foods

arepas

pabellón criollo

coffee

golfeado

arepas

Many people drink coffee. A *golfeado* is a sweet sticky bun with cheese!

Carnival is popular in Venezuela. Music and parades fill the streets.

Carnival

Families gather on New Year's Eve. Some people eat 12 grapes at midnight for luck! Venezuelans love to **celebrate** together.

Venezuela Facts

Size:
352,144 square miles
(912,050 square kilometers)

Population:
31,250,306 (2024)

National Holiday:
Independence Day (July 5)

Main Language:
Spanish

Capital City:
Caracas

Famous Face

Name: Evelyn Miralles

Famous For: businesswoman and former engineer at NASA

Religions

- none: 14%
- other: 6%
- Protestant: 32%
- Roman Catholic: 48%

Top Landmarks

Mount Roraima

National Pantheon of Venezuela

Waraira Repano National Park

Glossary

backgrounds—people's experiences, knowledge, and family histories

celebrate—to do something special or fun for a big event, occasion, or holiday

grasslands—lands covered with grasses and other soft plants with few bushes or trees

highlands—areas where the land is high above sea level

indigenous—related to people originally from an area

plains—large areas of flat land

rain forests—thick, green forests that receive a lot of rain

Roman Catholic—people belonging or relating to the Christian church that is led by the pope

unique—one of a kind

To Learn More

AT THE LIBRARY

Bellante, Claudia. *The Amazing Students of Venezuela*. Northampton, Mass.: Interlink Publishing Group, 2023.

Birdoff, Ariel Factor. *Venezuela*. New York, N.Y.: Bearport Publishing, 2019.

Grack, Rachel. *Jaguars*. Minneapolis, Minn.: Bellwether Media, 2019.

ON THE WEB

FACTSURFER

Factsurfer.com gives you a safe, fun way to find more information.

1. Go to www.factsurfer.com.

2. Enter "Venezuela" into the search box and click 🔍.

3. Select your book cover to see a list of related content.

Index

Angel Falls, 7
animals, 5, 10, 11
baseball, 15
capital (see Caracas)
Caracas, 4, 5
Carnival, 18, 19
cities, 12
coast, 6, 9
dry season, 8
food, 16, 17, 19
grasslands, 6
highlands, 6, 9
joropo, 14
languages, 12
map, 5
mountains, 6, 9
music, 14, 18
New Year's Eve, 19
people, 12, 15, 17, 19

plains, 6
rain forests, 6
river, 6, 11
Roman Catholic, 12
say hello, 13
soccer, 15
South America, 4
Spanish, 12
telenovelas, 15
Venezuela facts, 20–21
wet season, 8

The images in this book are reproduced through the courtesy of: Seventov, front cover; Sherif Ashraf 22, p. 3; Alejandro Solo, pp. 4-5; simonkr, p. 6; Photo Spirit, pp. 6-7; mundosemfim, pp. 8-9; Felix M. Hidalgo, p. 9; Henk Boogard, p. 10; Luis Zabala, p. 11 (ursine howler monkey); reisegraf.ch, p. 11 (jaguar); Jazmine Thomas, p. 11 (black spot piranha); Dirk M. de Boer, p. 11 (Venezuelan troupial); OsmanFernandez/ Wikipedia, p. 12; Amilciar Gualdron, pp. 12-13; JUAN BARRETO/ Getty, p. 14; A.PAES, pp. 14-15; Conde, p. 15; Civil, p. 16 (*arepas*); AS Foodstudio, p. 16 (*pabellón criollo*); Giovani Dressler, p. 16 (coffee); nehophoto, p. 16 (*golfeado*); Hello World Stock Library/ Alamy, p. 17; YURI CORTEZ/ Getty, pp. 18-19; Danii Belyay/ Alamy, p. 20 (flag); Stintegrity/ Wikipedia, p. 20 (Evelyn Miralles); Alexandree, p. 21 (Mount Roraima); Ipek Morel, p. 21 (National Pantheon of Venezuela); Paolo Costa, p. 21 (Waraira Repano National Park); Rahj.Photography, p. 22.